9/20 | | 7PN

PRU'S DIARY

EGMONT

We bring stories to life

First published in 2018 in North America / United States by Little,
Brown and Company. This edition published in Great Britain in 2020
by Egmont UK Limited
2 Minster Court, 10th floor, London EC3R 7BB
www.egmont.co.uk

ISBN 978 1 4052 9918 3
71169/001
Printed in the United Kingdom

Cover Design by Ching Chan

Egmont takes its responsibility to the planet
and its inhabitants very seriously. We aim to use papers from well-
managed forests run by responsible suppliers.

DREAMWORKS
Spirit
RIDING FREE

Pru's Diary

PRU

STACIA DEUTSCH

Diary Entry

Dear New Diary,

It's been almost four weeks that I've been on the road with Lucky and Abigail and <u>El Circo Dos Grillos</u>. The time has flown by. This is the most amazing adventure of my whole life. When Abigail and I went to Lucky's house and discovered that she'd run away to join the circus, I couldn't have imagined that I'd join the circus, too.

Who'd have guessed?! Me! A clown?! I used to have <u>terrible</u> stage fright and now it's pretty easy for me to perform with Boomerang. As Abigail says (over and over), 'Who'd've thunk it?'

I know ... all this clowning around should be impossible for someone like me, but Boomerang makes it easy. That horse has been a clown his whole life, even if he didn't know it. The first time we were in the ring together, the performance was an accident. He got away from me, I tried to catch him ... after a few bumps and falls ... ta-da — we were a clown show. Now we're professionals, with costumes and decorations and a fan club, real <u>live</u> applauding and cheering fans. <u>WOW!</u>

Abigail and Lucky are so supportive that they gave me this book to write down my creative ideas for the show ... but I think I'll use it for something more. I have a secret to share and I figure a diary can't tell anyone else ... right? I'm not complaining or anything. I mean, I really love it here and being with Abigail and Lucky all the time is the best thing in the world. The work is hard — setting up shows and breaking them down makes my muscles ache, but it's also really fun and seeing the circus come together is amazing. The food off the truck is good. I love seeing new parts of the country and have been to beautiful places I never even imagined! Every day is new and exciting, but the thing is ...

And this is hard to admit ...

But ...

I miss home. I mean, when Abigail and I discovered fluffy pillows, instead of Lucky, in

Lucky's bed, we left Miradero
that very same day. We didn't
pack our own clothes or say
goodbye to anyone. I left some
notes, but it's not the same as
giving someone a big hug when
you go away and saying, 'See
you later ... '

My mum and dad know where
I am and we send letters, but
it's not like being in Miradero,
sleeping in my own room or
working in the stable, mucking
out Chica Linda's very own stall.

I have a letter from my dad that
always cheers me up. Since this
is the first entry in my new diary,

I am going to put it here so I can
read it whenever I want. The letter
is a little torn and dirty since I've
read it a million times already, but
it makes me super happy.

Pru,

Your mother and I understand that you're out on the range, helping your friends on an adventure. We were worried at first ... and might have grounded you for a year, if we'd only known your plans. But since we didn't get that chance, we're satisfied with knowing that we raised you well and trust that you know how to make it for a while on your own.

Thanks for letting us know you arrived safely at the circus. We want you to know how very proud we are of you.

Your mum and I agree that
every foal needs to learn to walk
on it's own legs. You've seen how
it happens in the stable or in the
field. The newborn babe stumbles
as he tries to stand for the first
time. He takes a few wobbly steps.
Then he rises to his full height
and joins the herd.

You're not a babe anymore, but
you're still like the foal. You may
stumble, but know this, Pru —
your friends and family are behind
you to help steady your legs. Rise
up, Pru Granger and walk tall in
that circus of yours.

We look forward to the day you come back home. We'll build a campfire and gather round to hear your wild stories from the country Maybe you can show us your clown act? We'd all like that.

You should also know, Pru, that I hired Turo to do some of your chores while you're gone. He wants you and Abigail and Lucky to know he built you all a surprise in the horse stalls for when you get back.

That's all from Miradero.
Dad
PS: Your mum says, 'Eat your vegetables.'

My dad's not a super-emotional
guy, but he sure does write a nice
letter! And I wonder what Turo did
in the horses' stalls. I'm sure Spirit,
Boomerang and Chica Linda will
love it – whatever it is.

Okay, Diary, that's enough
for today.

Lucky and Abigail are waiting for
me. We've got to get ready for our
next stop—Durango City! I can't
wait to show off what Boomerang
and I have planned. This show's
going to be the best one yet.

CHAPTER 1

Durango City was a small town in a valley between two large mountains. Pru had seen mountains before, there were several high peaks around Miradero, but none as high as these. She had to shield her eyes against the sunlight to look up and even then, she could barely see their high snowcapped tops.

'Wow,' Pru said on a long breath. She was thrilled they'd have a few days in town. Sunset against those peaks might be a highlight of this whole trip. She could only imagine what kind of wild horses lived …

'Stop daydreaming, Pru.' Abigail's voice jolted Pru back to reality.

'How did you know that I was daydreaming?' Pru asked, looking over at Abigail, who was loading boxes onto a small cart. Boomerang was tied to the cart, ready to pull the supplies.

Abigail laughed. 'Glazed over eyes. Blank expression. Bit of drool. I invented that face.' She pointed at the tall stacks of boxes sitting nearby. 'I can't wait to get these cartons delivered so I can stare at those mountains, too! Did you try to imagine what kind of horses lived on the peaks?'

Pru laughed. 'You know me too well.'

'Mustangs, of course,' Lucky said, coming up to her friends and joining the conversation. She was riding bareback on Spirit. Looking down at her friends, she said, 'Wild mustangs. Are there any other options?'

'I was thinking unicorns,' Abigail replied.

'I mean, if I were a unicorn and didn't want anyone to see me, I'd find a home high up on a mountain where no one would ever catch me.' She added, 'See the way the sun sparkles against the snow? You can see bright-coloured flecks. Those are definitely the outlines of pink unicorns with purple horns. They're flickering because they are playing.'

'Unicorns? I'm pretty sure they don't exist, Abigail,' Pru said, moving closer to Boomerang to rub his nose.

'And if they did, are unicorns even horses?' Lucky asked.

'Of course they're horses, silly.' Abigail put her hands on her hips. 'Everyone knows they're horses. Aren't they, Boomerang?' she asked her own horse, who pulled back against the rope she was holding and seemed to nod his head.

'See?' Abigail told her friends. 'Boomerang knows I'm right.' She pointed to the mountain. 'I bet there is an amazing unicorn herd up there. We should explore … '

'Señoritas!' It was Fito. He owned *El Circo Dos Grillos* with his wife, Estrella. 'Less chatting. More working.'

'I'll help them,' Solana said. She was a circus performer and good friends with Pru, Abigail and Lucky.

Pru sighed. She was certain there were no unicorns on the mountain, but still, she'd have liked an adventure. Unfortunately, there'd be no time to explore those beautiful mountains. Not on this trip. These few days in Durango City were packed with things to do: They had to set up for all the performances fast because the circus had its first show that very same night. The next day there was an afternoon and an evening show. And the day after that, they'd pack it up to move on.

With one last look at the mountain peaks, Pru told Abigail, 'If you lead Boomerang and the cart to the performance area, I'll get Chica Linda and meet you there. We'll unload.'

'I'll stay here with Solana,' Lucky suggested. 'We can organise the boxes to reload the cart.' She hopped off Spirit's back. 'Spirit can help us move things around.' The magnificent horse dipped his head to push a box with his nose. It moved slowly towards Boomerang's cart.

Lucky grabbed the crate and looked inside. 'Costumes for Solana's trapeze act,' she reported. She lifted up a short red dress with sequins and a matching parasol.

'Oh, that's my favourite dress,' Solana cooed. 'Okay, Boomerang, take good care of the deliveries.'

Boomerang whinnied and started to move forward, dragging the cart, but without Solana's box.

'Hang on!' Lucky called, running after the cart. She caught up and gave the box to Abigail, who put it on top of all the other boxes.

'Okay, Boomerang, let's get to work!' Abigail took one last look up at the mountain peaks. 'Oh, look, did you see that? It was a green unicorn! I'm sure of it. The sparkle in the snow was the same colour as an avocado.'

'Are you sure?' Pru squinted into the distance as Lucky shook her head.

'Positive,' Abigail said while tightening her grip on Boomerang's lead line. 'Pru, Lucky, Solana – quick – make a wish! Green unicorns

16

are rare and kinda like genies. They make wishes come true!'

Pru and Lucky glanced at each other. Lucky shrugged.

'No harm in wishing,' Lucky said. She closed her eyes.

Solana took a turn.

Green unicorns? Wishes? Pru didn't buy it, so she moved her lips a bit but didn't make a wish.

'*Whew*,' Abigail said, heading towards the big white tent that was being built a short distance away. 'We might never see a green unicorn again – that was lucky!' She glanced at her friend Lucky and laughed. 'We have Lucky down here and more luck on the mountain. Things are looking fortunate for us in Durango City!' Whistling to herself, Abigail led Boomerang off.

Chica Linda was in the temporary corral the circus folks set up for the horses. Pru hurried to the tack truck and grabbed a saddle blanket, a saddle and reins. There wasn't time to groom Chica Linda now; she'd brush her down later.

'Hey, Chica Linda,' Pru said while tossing the blanket over her horse's back. She rubbed Chica Linda's neck and explained, 'Time to get set up for tonight's show. Abigail and Boomerang are going to leave the boxes for us to sort through.' Chica Linda stood still while Pru tightened the saddle strap and made sure it was secure. 'Are you sure you don't want to perform?' Pru always asked. The clown show was her act with Boomerang. Chica Linda didn't ever seem to want to be in the show.

Her horse shook her head and backed away.

'Okay,' Pru said, 'but let me know if you change your mind.'

18

'Are you talking to that horse?' A tall girl approached the corral. She was about Pru's age but looked a lot older. Her dark hair was tied back in a high, neat bun. Pru had never seen this girl before.

'Uh, yeah,' she said timidly. 'We're friends.'

The girl snorted. 'Sure you are. Girls can't be friends with horses.'

'Yes, they can,' Pru said. She looked around. There was no one else nearby. The girl was giving off a bad impression, but still, Pru was going to be polite. She cleared her throat and stood a little straighter. 'Hi. I'm Pru.'

'Are you with this sorry excuse for a circus, Pru?' the girl asked, not introducing herself.

'It's a really good circus,' Pru told her, staying positive. 'Are you coming to the show tonight? You'd have a good time, I promise.'

'I saw it,' she said in a rude tone.

'What do you mean?' Pru asked while

19

buckling Chica Linda's bridle. She'd never seen this girl before.

'We're on the same circuit,' she said. Then she added, 'My family is in the other circus. We're leaving today.' The girl turned her eyes towards a wide-open area on the other side of town.

Pru hadn't noticed it before, but there was a circus tent there. It was being taken down, while their circus was setting up.

'It's not the first time we've overlapped,' the girl said. 'Usually, though, we are ready to go when you arrive. In the last town, we were running late. I'm sure you didn't notice, but I hung around to watch your act.'

Pru needed to go help Abigail. Boomerang's cart would be at the performance area already. She had the sinking feeling that the girl had nothing nice to say, but still, she couldn't help asking, 'What did you think?'

'You'll never be as good as we are,' the girl said as Pru slipped up onto Chica Linda's back. 'The audience won't clap as loudly. Or cheer as enthusiastically. And I bet that no one will want your autograph.'

'Really?' Pru gave a long hard look at the girl, then climbed down from Chica Linda's back. 'What's your name?'

'Catalina,' she replied, puffing out her chest, 'from the *Circus Libre*.'

'I personally guarantee that our circus is just as good as yours,' Pru said, stepping forward. 'Better even.'

'No chance,' Catalina said. 'We're the best circus in the country.'

'Let me tell you about the best circ—' Pru started, when suddenly Abigail and Lucky appeared, rushing to her.

'Pru, where were you?' Lucky asked, glancing from Pru to Catalina and back.

'We've been waiting for you,' Abigail said. 'I need the cart for another load and Boom—' Abigail stopped herself. 'Who's your new friend?'

'She's not my friend,' Pru said firmly. 'This is Catalina and she thinks her circus is better than ours.'

'You told her she's wrong?' Lucky asked, eyeing Catalina warily.

Pru nodded.

'Great! Then let's go.' Lucky grabbed Pru's arm while Abigail took Chica Linda's reins. 'There's nothing more to say.'

'But—' Pru protested as they left Catalina standing alone by the horse corral. Catalina winked at Pru and that made Pru even more determined to prove herself. She told Lucky and Abigail, 'She said we were a 'sorry excuse for a circus'! We have to show her how great our circus is. We have to prove we're better.'

'How would we ever do that?' Lucky asked Pru. 'They're leaving. We're here now. And we will never see that girl again ... So none of this even matters, really.'

'Plus, we aren't going to have the best circus if we don't help set up,' Abigail said. 'Forget about her, Pru. There's so much to do!' She shouted out towards the performance area, 'We're coming, Boomerang!'

'But—' Pru glanced over her shoulder. Catalina was gone. With a big sigh, Pru turned her attention to the bustling circus in front of her and said,' I don't know how, but somehow I have to show that girl she's wrong about us.'

After the evening show, Pru signed more autographs than she'd ever signed before. Her hand hurt from signing so many.

She had added a trick with Boomerang
that made the audience howl with laughter.
Boomerang pushed a ball with his nose and
knocked Pru down as if she were a bowling
pin. Pru pretended to be mad at the horse, but
it was an act. They did the same thing again
and again and the audience cracked up every
time. She loved the way the audience laughed
with her.

'If only Catalina could have seen this
crowd!' Pru said to herself as she waved
goodbye to the last two boys in her
autograph line.

'Come on,' Lucky said to Pru. 'Let's clean
up fast, then go celebrate tonight's great
show.'

'I helped the cook make cupcakes in the
camp oven,' Abigail said proudly. 'Since
Boomerang is helping you, I had Chica Linda
help me. They're extra delicious.'

Pru wondered what exactly Chica Linda had done to help bake. Maybe Chica Linda had culinary skills she didn't know about. Did she wash her hooves before entering the kitchen?

Just before Pru went to organise costumes and props for the next show, two young girls came running up to her with blank paper in their hands.

'Can you sign this for me?' one girl asked. Her pigtails shook as she spoke. When Pru autographed the paper, she gasped. 'You're the most famous clown I ever met!'

The other girl thrust her own blank paper into Pru's hand. 'Sign this and I'll keep it safe all the way to Miradero.'

Pru began to sign the page, then her hand stalled. She wasn't sure she'd heard right. 'Where are you going?' she asked.

'Miradero,' the girl said. 'My family is

visiting there next. We're on vacation and people say it's the most beautiful town in the country.'

Pru looked up at the mountains behind her, towering over the horizon and thought about the girl's words for a long moment. 'You're right,' she said at last. There was a tinge of homesickness in her voice. 'Miradero is the most beautiful town I've ever seen.'

Pru brushed aside the feeling and finished the autograph. 'Be sure to get some ice cream and say hi to Mr Winthrop for us all! He owns the ice cream shop.' Pru added with a wink, 'He can be a bit of a grump, but he'll give you extra sprinkles if you ask.'

The two girls excitedly skipped off, holding their autographs close to their hearts.

Pru stared after them for a long moment, wondering if she should have made other suggestions, or maybe she could have asked them to talk to her parents for her. It was too late. They were gone. She turned her attention back to her friends.

'So, Abigail,' Pru said, 'tell me more about these cupcakes.'

Diary Entry

Dear Diary,

This morning, I had the most brilliant idea.

I think I should do a flip off a trampoline and land with flair on a horse's back.

The idea was so incredible that I hurried to the corral to ask Chica Linda if she wanted to be in the show. She's been refusing to be part of the circus, so I've been doing the clown act with Boomerang. I thought that maybe this idea would get her excited. If she was willing, I could land on her back. The crowd would love it.

Of course, when I asked, Chica Linda gave me a look as if I were crazy. There was no way I was going to flip and land on <u>her</u> back.

I told her I was sure that Boomerang would be into the idea. In fact, Boomerang would probably love jumping on a trampoline himself, if there were one big enough.

Chica Linda snorted.

I told her to let me know if she changed her mind.

If the trampoline idea doesn't work out, I have a few other ideas up my clown sleeve that are all for Boomerang. Maybe I could pretend I don't know anything about horses and try to put a saddle on Boomerang while he's moving. Or teach Boomerang to throw a baseball. Or ...

Hang on, Lucky, Solana and Abigail are here to report big news. Be right back ...

U U U

Well, Diary, it turns out the caravan is making a surprise stop on the way to our next show in Triple Creek.

Fito and Estrella have been sneaking around and whispering a lot lately, so we all knew something was up, but we thought it was something small — like changing the ticket colours or adding food colouring to the popcorn.

But Solana heard from the lion tamer, who heard from an acrobat, who heard from the fire-eater, who overheard Fito and Estrella saying that we are going to Low Shores.

Before I could ask why that was important, Solana blurted out that there is going to be a gathering and exhibition festival for all the travelling circuses!

<u>WOW!</u>

Abigail claimed it was her unicorn wish come true, that she'd wished we could go to a festival and now we were!

Can you believe that Abigail spent her lucky unicorn wish on the idea of a festival? Sounds silly to me ... especially since unicorn wishes aren't a thing. But since she seems sure that the unicorn wish is the reason

we are heading to a festival, it
kind of makes me wonder ...

However it happened, this is
great news. I mean, I've been
in riding exhibitions before, so a
circus one must be similar, right?
At an exhibition, riders get to
show off their skills, not in
competition, but for fun. Since we
haven't seen other circus acts
yet, I'm excited to see what the
other clowns will be doing.

The pressure is on. If I'm going
to the exhibition, then it's gotta be
the most amazing clown act I've
ever done. I don't know what it
is going to be yet, but my amazing

friends offered some new ideas
for the show. They suggested:

- I could ride while juggling
  pies (that was Abigail's idea).
- Boomerang could ride a bike
  (also Abigail's idea).
- I could teach Boomerang a
  dance (Solana's idea).
- I could teach Boomerang
  to play a musical instrument
  (Lucky's idea).

Of everything we thought of so
far, Lucky's might be my favourite
idea, but what instrument? And
how would I teach a horse to

play? I have to think more about that.

If Durango City was the best show I've done so far, this one is going to be even better than that!

CHAPTER 2

El Circo Dos Grillos was one of the last circuses to arrive at Low Shores. The broad meadow was nestled between two large lakes that glistened in the evening sun.

The caravan pulled into a wide-open space that had a small sign in the centre, welcoming them. Each circus had its own well-marked area.

Judging by the tents and the flags, Pru could see that there were twelve circuses there. Her heart began to race. She was excited to see the other acts but, at the same time, nervous about her own! The billowing performance tents stretched out in all directions. Smaller tents for sleeping or practice dotted the fields in bright, mismatched colours. Even though *El Circo Dos Grillos* didn't have a big tent – they performed in the open air – once they were done setting up their sleeping and practice tents, the last patch of grass would be covered.

The sounds of chatter and music, the howls and brays and neighs of performing animals and the smells of a thousand different foods filled the air.

'This is the most incredible place I've ever seen! We gotta explore,' Lucky said.

'We can't,' Pru said. There was always so much work to do when the caravan first pulled into a town.

Pru had no doubt that before the night was over, she'd be even more tired than she already was. She'd been staying up late, writing show ideas in her journal, thinking of ways to improve her act for the exhibition. There were a few good ideas in her notebook but nothing amazing and she wanted this performance to be *amazing*. Her own performance was on the last day of the three-day festival, so Pru still had some time. But if an idea didn't come to her soon, she'd never have time to practise with Boomerang.

'Pru's right,' Abigail told Lucky. 'Work comes first. We can go look around tomorrow.' Abigail gazed over Lucky's shoulder at a spot where someone had set off small fireworks and sighed. 'Sometimes it's hard being mature and very grown-up.'

Lucky stared out at the fireworks and pinched her lips together.

'Lucky ... don't even think about it,' Pru warned. 'We have to stay with the circus.'

'Come, girls.' Estrella called them to gather near the marker sign.

'*Buenas tardes*, amigos.' Fito stood on a small ladder so he could address the entire circus staff. He had to shout over the sounds coming from the other circuses in the meadow. 'It's late and I know you are all tired after the long days of travel. Leave the supplies for now,' Fito told them all. 'We'll set up the main performance area and a smaller practice tent tomorrow. Relax. Estrella and I will set up the corral and feed the horses. No one works. Tonight, you all should have fun and explore.'

There was a cheer from the circus performers. It seemed that everyone wanted to find out more about the gathering.

'My unicorn wish just came true,' Lucky told Pru and Abigail with a laugh.

'What did you wish for?' Abigail asked, clearly excited that the unicorn wishes were working.

'*Adventure!*' Lucky cheered, taking her friends' arms and dragging them to where Solana was standing. 'Come on, Solana, we're off!'

As they headed towards the loudest music and the brightest tent, Abigail asked Pru, 'What was your unicorn wish?'

Pru shook her head playfully. 'I can't tell you or it won't come true.' Truth was, Pru hadn't made one, but she didn't want to make Abigail feel bad.

It was as if Abigail read her mind. 'Don't be a doubter, Pru. A wish will come true for you, you'll see.' With that, and before Pru could protest, Abigail skipped ahead, linking arms with Lucky and Solana.

'Come on, Pru,' Solana called over her shoulder. 'Catch up.'

'Yeah, Pru, catch up.' A mocking voice came from somewhere behind her.

'Huh?' Pru stopped and turned around. There, in the rising moonlight, stood a girl. She was alone in the field. Her hair was wild. Her jeans and T-shirt were loose fitting and well worn. Pru almost didn't recognise her, but then – she winked.

'Catalina,' Pru muttered under her breath. Louder she asked, 'What are you doing here?'

'It's a circus gathering.' Catalina stated the obvious. 'I'm here to perform, just like you.'

Pru knew that Abigail, Lucky and Solana were getting farther away. Eventually they'd notice she wasn't with them.

'What exactly do you do in this amazing circus of yours?' Pru asked, squinting hard at Catalina.

'I'm a clown,' Catalina told her.

Pru was surprised. Catalina didn't seem the goofing-around type. Then again, maybe Pru didn't seem that type, either.

'Me too,' Pru responded. 'Will you be performing?'

Catalina huffed. 'Of course. Are you?'

Pru imitated her huff and repeated, 'Of course.'

'You might as well not show up,' Catalina said. 'I already warned you that we're the best circus in the country.'

Pru knew if Lucky and Abigail were there, they'd tell her to forget about Catalina and come explore instead. There was no real way to prove *El Circo Dos Grillos* was better than *Circus Libre*, so why bother? The exhibition was all about sharing shows and having fun. There were no awards or trophies, so why was Pru feeling so feisty?

'It's not a competition,' Pru declared, though she was feeling awfully competitive.

'It sort of is,' Catalina countered.

That caught Pru's attention. 'What do you mean?'

'Lydia Sebastian is coming,' Catalina said, in a tone that seemed to expect that Pru knew who that was already. At Pru's confused look, Catalina offered, 'She's a reporter for the newspaper.'

Pru shrugged. She still didn't know the name.

'Ugh.' Catalina exhaled, as if telling Pru about Lydia Sebastian was the last thing on Earth she wanted to do. 'She's going to write an article that will showcase only the *best* acts,' Catalina explained. 'I've always been chosen.' She added, 'And I always get a photo, too.'

Catalina was getting under Pru's skin.

'Maybe this year I'll get my picture in the newspaper,' Pru suggested. 'It could happen.'

'No way,' Catalina said. 'Not only is my act the best clown act, but I've known *Lydia*, the writer, for years. We're both from Copper Springs. Her youngest sister was in my class at school; that makes us practically friends.' Catalina gave a small laugh and declared, 'I'm going to prove to you that I'm the better clown, right here in front of Every. Single. Circus. My name will be in the paper!'

Pru's blood was boiling. Now the exhibition *was* a competition and she was going to do whatever she had to in order to be the one in the newspaper!

'You're on!' Pru told Catalina. 'See you in the big tent!'

Pru turned and stormed away, leaving Catalina in the field. But stomping off wasn't satisfying. By the time she reached her friends, Pru's face was on fire and her blood was hot.

She told them what happened.

'Pru, don't let Catalina get under your skin,' Lucky said.

'Yeah, that would be terrible,' said Abigail. 'I mean, skin is stretchy and everything, but two people can't fit in one body.'

Lucky snapped her head to Abigail with a grossed-out look.

'Oh, that wasn't literal?' Abigail shrugged. 'I'll get it next time.'

'It's too late,' Pru said. 'Now I have to show Catalina that I'm a great clown, too.' She groaned. 'But how? You know, I was already planning to do something special, but I don't have an idea yet.'

'I've been thinking that you should do your usual show,' Lucky said. 'It gets a million laughs and everyone loves it.'

'You can do the new bowling-ball part, too,' Solana said. 'The crowd in Durango City thought it was hysterical. I swear I saw a little boy laugh so hard that he cried.'

'Oh, that was because I spilled his popcorn,' Abigail started, then corrected herself. 'And because he was laughing really hard.'

'I don't know,' Pru said, staring out at the endless rows of tents spread all around them. 'Tonight's my last night of fun. Tomorrow, the work begins. Boomerang and I are going to practise until our routine is a winner.'

'Well, then,' Lucky said, clear that she couldn't talk Pru out of her determination. 'We better get started! We have to make tonight the best adventure ever!'

They began the night by going into the nearest circus encampment, where a band was playing and people were dancing.

Pru danced with her friends until her feet couldn't dance a step more.

Diary Entry

Dear Diary,

One quick note to you, one quick letter home, then I'm off to get Boomerang and start practising. I haven't come up with a brilliant idea yet, seeing as I have been awake for only twenty minutes, but today's the day! Some stroke of genius is going to hit me and I'll be ready when it does.

In the meantime, I have to tell you, last night was so much fun. We started at the Circus of the

South's campsite and that is where we danced. They have a big performance tent that is taller than any of the other tents around. Even Solana said that she'd be nervous about how high up their tightrope walkers are above the ground. The band that was there last night was playing Southern-style music with a fast rhythm and snappy beat. I'd never danced fast like that with a partner before and Miz Prescott might have fainted if she saw us, but several performers from their circus taught us the steps.

At the next tent, the Russian River Circus showed us more dance steps, but this time from <u>Russia</u>! I didn't know anything about Russia, but now I have two future pen pals from there.

Lucky picked the next tent to visit. It was the smallest at the gathering. To our surprise, it was a circus without any people acts. They have dogs, horses and even llamas, but no people, except the trainers – it was like a petting zoo. I can't wait to see what these animals do for a show!

We didn't visit everyone. It got
too late and I was fading into a
puddle of tired Pru. There are so
many circuses here, I can't wait
to see as many of the exhibitions
as I can. Between my own
practices, of course.

On the way home, we stopped
near a quiet tent. It wasn't as
big as the Circus of the South's,
but it was bigger than the
Amazing Animals'. It was silent.
There wasn't a party there
and I wondered if their whole
group was out exploring.
Or maybe this circus had just
arrived, too?

I peeked in through the flap
and there was one person inside.
Alone.

It was Catalina. I couldn't tell
what she was doing, but she was
sitting in the stands, looking at
something in her hand and
frowning. She didn't see me (at
least I don't think so).

Lucky tugged me away. Abigail
told me not to let Catalina ruin
my fun night. And Solana told me
that she heard that our camp, even
without a tent, had built a huge
bonfire and was offering fire-roasted
corncobs to anyone who visited.

Actually, Solana confessed that her wish on the green unicorn had been for the roasted corncobs. They're her favourite!

For a second, I considered inviting Catalina, but then I remembered how rude she'd been when I first met her, so I didn't. Plus, she's the competition, after all.

We hurried back to our own camp and snacked until we were stuffed full.

It was a great night. And now, the work begins. No distractions for Pru. I'm staying super-focussed

on the task. Oh, I did learn
something else last night — that's
why I have to write home. I
want to tell them the news ...
   More later!

Dear Mum and Dad,

Last night was an amazing night at the circus. We are at a gathering of all the travelling circuses. I'm seeing new acts, learning about other kinds of circuses and, best of all, making new friends.

Lucky and Abigail are helping me with a new act for the exhibition at the gathering. We haven't come up with something great yet, but we will. That brings me to my big news:

There's a reporter here and she's going to do an article on

the best acts. Last night, at the Russian River Circus tent, I learned that the reporter is famous. She'll send the article to all the regional presses, including Miradero's newspaper, the <u>Bugle</u>! So you know what that means?

I gotta work hard and be the best act ... so you can see me in the paper!

All those competitions I did in Miradero have prepared me for this one — so thanks, Mum and Dad. You both always help me be the best Pru I can be.

I miss you both very much. I miss the barn and the ramada and even when Dad makes me fix the fence. I miss putting Chica Linda in her own stall at night (even though she's okay here in the corral). I miss sleeping in my own room. I even miss Mum's green-bean casserole (I'm eating vegetables, Mum, but they just aren't as good). I'll admit sometimes I get a little homesick thinking about everything I miss.

But life here is good, too. So don't you worry about me!

Oh, I gotta go. Lucky and Abigail are here with Spirit, Boomerang and Chica Linda. We're going to the practice tent and they're going to help me with my act. I perform in three days. Wish me luck!

Your daughter,
Pru

CHAPTER 3

Pru forgot to mail the letter. She put it in Boomerang's saddlebag, meaning to mail it later, but she forgot. The next day, when she went to find it and put on the postage, the letter was gone.

She didn't have time to write it over again, so she decided that the photo in the newspaper would have to be a surprise for her parents – she focussed on clowning around.

'Hiya, Pru.' Lucky came into the practice tent. Everything was ready for the circus now; the entire caravan was unpacked and Pru had signed up for 'tent time,' since she wasn't the only one who needed to get prepared for a show.

Pru grunted at Lucky. Her time in the tent was running out and she'd barely done anything.

'You look frustrated,' Lucky said. 'Can I help?'

'I'm here,' Abigail said, popping her head into the tent. 'I was going to help Solana with her practice tightrope, but I got tangled in the rope.' The practice tightrope was a long cord tied between two raised ladders. Not as high as the real one above the audience, but if you fell in practice, it wasn't very far to the ground.

Abigail went on. 'Solana told me to take a break while she untangled it.' Abigail shrugged. 'She said she'd come get me when she's ready for my help.' Pinching her lips together, Abigail said, 'The rope was pretty tangled and I kind of knocked over one of the ladders, too. It might be a while.'

'Or never,' Lucky whispered to Pru, who struggled not to laugh.

'Oh, she'll come,' Abigail said confidently, having overheard them.

Boomerang was standing nearby, waiting for Pru to tell him what to do.

Pru thought about home. When she was learning to ride, her dad would laugh when she fell – as long as she wasn't hurt – and that would make her laugh, too. Giggling about mistakes made learning fun. She missed her dad's deep and heavy laughter.

'I haven't fallen off a horse in a while, but maybe I should add that to the act,' Pru suggested.

'Sounds painful,' Lucky said. 'There must be something else you can do for the show.' She rubbed her chin as she struggled for ideas.

The girls were standing quietly in a circle in the centre of the tent when the flap opened.

'Chica Linda!' Pru exclaimed. 'How'd you get here?'

'She must have jumped the corral fence,' Abigail said. And just then Spirit entered the tent. 'It was a breakout!'

Lucky giggled and ran to hug her horse. 'Okay,' she told Pru. 'We're all here. Give us your best idea.'

Pru opened her diary to where she'd written her brainstorming list.

'No, no, no.' She didn't even read the bad ones out loud. 'The only half-decent idea here is to teach Boomerang to play an instrument.'

'A one-horse band? That's easy, since he can already sing,' Abigail said.

'Huh?' Pru and Lucky both asked at the same time.

'Go on, Boomerang. Show them how you sing,' Abigail told her horse.

The girls waited.

The tent was silent.

'He's shy,' Abigail assured them. 'Let's try the instrument idea instead.'

'Maybe he can play drums with his tail?' Lucky suggested. She ran to the storage area and brought back two plastic buckets, a small yellow one and a bigger grey one.

'If he can play, I'll paint them,' Abigail said. 'Fancy buckets for my fancy horse!'

Boomerang nickered and Abigail kissed his nose.

'Okay, you majestic steed,' she said. 'Let's hear your beat.'

Abigail tried to turn Boomerang backward

so his tail would swish the bucket, but he refused to budge. She moved the buckets around near his backside and he turned around to face them. 'This isn't working,' she complained.

'Let me try,' Pru told her. 'He's gotta do it with me anyway.' She showed Boomerang how to swish his tail down onto the bucket by grabbing hold of his tail and thumping it on the bucket bottom. It made a banging sound that reverberated through the tent. But once she set down the bucket, Boomerang wandered away, uninterested.

'We're gonna need a new idea,' Lucky said. The girls huddled to think of something else, but they couldn't come up with anything.

Estrella poked her head in the tent. 'Girls, time's up. The acrobats need to prepare their act.'

Pru nodded sadly. 'What am I going to do?' she moaned. 'No new ideas!'

'Your old ideas are working perfectly,' Abigail reminded her. 'You get more laughs than any other performer.'

Pru stared at her. 'I'm the clown.'

'I'm just saying,' Abigail said. 'Your act is fine just the way it is.'

'Fine?' Pru's frustration was rising. 'If I'm going to be in the newspaper, where all Miradero will see me, I have to be better than fine!' She took a deep breath and apologised to Abigail. 'I don't mean to yell; it's just that Catalina is in my head. It's as if we are competing, even though I know the circus isn't a competition.'

'I get that—' Lucky began, when suddenly a *boom-boom* drum sound filled the tent.

The girls looked over to find that Chica Linda was playing the bucket drums. She wasn't using her tail to make the sound, but rather her hooves. She'd hit one drum with her hoof, then turn slightly to hit the other one.

As Chica Linda figured out how to beat the drums, her rhythms got faster.

Pru rushed over to her. 'Chica Linda! You're amazing! Can you do that in the circus?'

Chica Linda quickly backed away from the drums and moved towards the tent flap, leaving the same way she'd entered.

'No, wait!' Pru hurried after her.

'That horse does *not* want to be in a circus,' Lucky told Abigail as they both got their own horses. 'She might be the best drumming horse in the country but there's no way she'll perform.'

'Can Spirit drum?' suggested Abigail.

'I'm not even going to ask,' said Lucky.

'Clowning around is not really Spirit's thing. We've gotta get Boomerang to do it.'

Abigail swung up on Boomerang's back. 'I think I'd have better luck convincing him to sing.'

'Looks as if we need something else for Pru and Boomerang to do,' Lucky said. 'Let's go for a ride and we can think more about it.'

They went to get Pru and found her, with Chica Linda, hiding behind a large painted truck from the Mexicali Circus.

'Why are you hid—' Lucky started.

'*Shhhh!*' Pru whispered.

Lucky and Abigail smushed next to Pru. The horses tried to tuck in, too, but it was crowded and they bumped one another.

Pru peeked out of the hiding spot. 'It's Catalina,' she whispered.

The girls and their horses all glanced around the truck. Abigail and Boomerang

bent to see from underneath in the gap
between the wheels.

'Who's she talking to?' Abigail asked.

Catalina was standing with a tall woman.
Dark skin. Brown hair. She had a pencil
tucked behind an ear and was holding a
notebook. Catalina leaned forward and
laughed at whatever the woman was saying.

'It's gotta be Lydia Sebastian,' Pru said.
She grunted. 'Catalina said she knew her.'

'Looks as if they're friends,' Lucky said.

'I know!' Pru blurted that a little loud,
drawing Catalina's attention. They all quickly
pulled back tighter into the hiding space.
Pru whispered, 'Catalina has an advantage
because she already knows Lydia and has
been in the paper before.' She put her hands
on her hips. 'That's why I have to do the best
show I've ever done!' Pru handed Abigail
Chica Linda's reins and took Boomerang's.

'Come on, Boomerang, there's no time to lose. We need to practise ... something.'

Pru began to walk away.

'We were going to go for a ride,' Lucky called after her.

'You'll have to go without me,' Pru said to her friends. 'Boomerang and I have too much to do to get ready.'

Diary Entry

Ideas

1. I ride sitting backward and juggle at the same time.
2. I put a lion's mane on Boomerang and try to repeat the lion tamer's show.
3. Horse ballet
4. Horse badminton
5. ~~≈≈≈≈≈~~ !!!!

Dear Diary,

I'm stuck. The first few ideas aren't bad, but for every one of them, I have a reason it won't work.

1. I can't juggle.
2. Lion taming — not my thing.
3. Would Boomerang wear a tutu? Where would I get one?
4. I stink at badminton.
5. Yeah ... I'm out of ideas.

Tomorrow is Friday. My act is the last one before the closing ceremony on Sunday. That means I have to stop being so negative and to convince Boomerang into one of those ideas — fast! Just one. Maybe the ballet. That seems the easiest, since I don't need to juggle.

Truth is, I'm no closer to coming up with the most awesome idea ever, but it's late and I promised Lucky and Abigail that I'd meet Solana with them and we'd all go out.

Tonight is the big welcome dinner for all the circuses.

All the circuses are bringing a food item from their region of

the country or spot in the world.
I never thought I'd want to travel
much outside of Miradero, but
being here and with the circus
gathering, has made me think
more about seeing the world.
I mean, I love my country and our
country foods. I hear the
Mexicali Circus performers
are making something called
sopaipillas — like puffy donuts with
honey. There's a trapeze group
from Greece that is bringing
spanakopita, which is a spinach
and cheese pie. The acrobats
from India are cooking up curry.

Chinese tumblers are bringing lo mein, a spicy noodle dish. And the Italian animal trainers are making pizza in a brick oven. I can't wait for that! Each circus is made up of so many people, from all different backgrounds and cultures and they each provide their own flair.

Of course, <u>El Circo Dos Grillos</u> is repeating our offering of delicious, fresh fire-roasted corncobs and on Abigail's insistence, adding s'mores, which have become a staple for late nights on our circus circuit. Everyone knows s'mores aren't a Mexican tradition, but we love them all the same.

Anyhoo, the foods, the people, the cultures — I definitely want to travel the world someday. Maybe the PALs can take our adventures around the globe! Wouldn't that be incredible? I'm not ready for it yet — but the day will come when I won't miss Mum's green-bean casserole so much and that's when I'll know I'm ready to go out, across the sea, with my friends.

For now, I am going to have

my world adventure here at the circus gathering.

I can't wait.

I think we should start with the treats at <u>El Circo Dos Grillos</u>'s campfire ...

CHAPTER 4

'This way!' Lucky pulled Pru's arm. She wanted to go into a colourful tent where loud music was booming.

'No, this way!' Abigail took Pru's other arm. She wanted to go into a quieter tent where artists were showing their new costume ideas.

Solana laughed as Pru was pulled tight, like a rope in tug-of-war.

'Help me,' Pru begged Solana. 'They're gonna rip off my arms!' They weren't really, but Pru didn't want to be in the middle of the fight.

'I vote for the big purple tent where the Clydesdale horses are kept,' Solana said, pointing at a large billowing tent in the distance.

'I hear horses!' Lucky cheered. She and Abigail both dropped Pru's arms and hurried towards the purple tent.

Pru and Solana followed.

Inside the purple tent, they were welcomed by the Circus on Wheels. The name meant they had a huge caravan and travelled great distances to perform. They'd had to cross a dangerous mountain range to get to this gathering.

Pru was excited by the way the Appaloosas pranced in unison around the circus ring, lifting their legs at the exact same time in perfect harmony. They pulled a truck and had a short parade before the circus ringmaster announced, 'This is just a sample of what you'll see our horses do during their exhibition performance!' He then reminded everyone that the grand opening ceremony of the circus gathering was the next night. It was the first time the public could see all the circuses in the same place. Pru couldn't wait – there were so many tents they'd already seen but so many they hadn't! This was her chance to catch a glimpse of everyone in the valley.

After the Appaloosas, Lucky wanted to go check up on Spirit. 'It'll just be a few minutes, then we can get back to exploring,' she told the others. Abigail wanted to go along, too. Pru wasn't worried about Chica Linda. There was something she wanted to do, but she was embarrassed, so if everyone left her alone for a few minutes, she could make a quick stop.

'Solana,' she said, turning to her friend, 'can you give an apple to Chica Linda for me?'

'I'd be glad to,' Solana said. 'But where are you going?'

'Uh.' Pru glanced around. 'The bathroom?' It sounded more like a question than a statement. 'The bathroom,' she corrected. 'Drank a lot of water today.' There were outhouses nearby.

'Pru,' Lucky gave her a serious eye.

'Oh, fine.' Pru admitted the truth. She could never lie to anyone, especially not her friends. 'I want to peek in on Catalina. I know she's working on something for the show and I just want to see what she's up to.' Catalina's circus tent was the opposite way from their own circus.

'We'll go with you,' Abigail suggested. 'We could be spies, like Boxcar Bonnie. I can get a magnifying glass and Lucky can write clues in a notebook. Oh, Pru, can we borrow your diary to use as a notebook? We'll give it back after we are done.'

'I'm not looking for clues,' Pru said. 'This isn't a mystery.'

'Besides, Bonnie's a detective,' Lucky explained. Boxcar Bonnie was the heroine of her favourite mystery novels. 'It's different from being a spy.' She considered it and added, 'Though she does sneak around sometimes.'

Pru paused, wondering if they all should go, but then she blurted out, 'I need to go on my own,' Pru told them. 'I'm just going to take a quick peek and I'll hurry back to the corral. We can go from there to get curry.'

'Yum,' Abigail said, rubbing her belly. 'I was there when they were cooking it. I might have had a taste ... or two.'

'Go,' Lucky told Pru. 'But you have to tell us everything.'

'I will,' Pru replied. 'I promise. Just a little look to see what she's up to. I think it'll take the pressure off me to come up with something new. Maybe I'm already better than her. I just gotta find out. I need to know!'

'Pru?' Solana had a question. 'What if Catalina is out enjoying the foods at the tents, exploring and having fun tonight – like us?'

'She's not,' Pru said, feeling assured. 'She's like me.' She looked at her friends. 'If I didn't have the most wonderful friends taking me around, I'd be back in our practice tent practising, too. I know she's there.'

Lucky, Abigail and Solana took off towards the horse corral, leaving Pru to her detective work. She told herself it wasn't a spy mission – just friendly snooping. Pru didn't feel bad. She actually assumed that Catalina had probably snuck by earlier to see what she was doing, too – only to discover that Pru wasn't doing anything but writing bad ideas in her diary!

Hopefully, Pru would feel more confident after seeing whatever Catalina was up to.

Pru heard the music before she reached Catalina's circus tent. It was ... awful. As if someone were banging on a piano with their forehead. *Slam, crash, bang.* She held her ears and shuddered.

'What is going on?' Pru quietly inched towards a slit in the tent fabric. She peeked through the slot and saw Catalina. 'I was right,' she whispered to herself. Catalina was there, alone, standing in front of a piano, practising ... but practising what? Pru moved to a larger gap in the tent where she could see better.

Now she could tell that Catalina was not alone. There was a horse with her. It was clearly a palomino, like Chica Linda, but darker in colour and a little smaller overall. Pru stuck her face almost all the way into the tent gap, struggling to hear what Catalina was saying to her horse.

'Come on, Milton, you know what to do.' Catalina pulled the horse's reins towards the piano. Pru could see that Milton was resisting. 'Come on, please?' Catalina begged. 'For me?'

Pru swallowed a laugh. Begging didn't generally work with horses.

Then there was the music. Pru had been right! Someone *was* banging their head on the piano. It was Catalina. She was showing Milton how to bang his own head on the keys.

'Oh!' Pru spoke so loudly she had to step back from the tent so Catalina wouldn't notice her there. When she felt the coast was clear, she leaned in again to confirm what she'd seen. It was true!

Catalina was stealing Pru's act. Well, okay, so Pru was trying to get Boomerang to play drums and Catalina was trying to get Milton to play piano – and they were both failing – but *still*! Getting the horses to play music for the clown act was the same thing!

Pru's head was spinning with questions:

Had Catalina seen Pru's act and decided it was a good idea and stolen it for herself?

Did they both just have the same idea?

Why wouldn't Milton play piano? Pru had to admit, that was a better idea than the drums. It would be easier to teach a horse to bang on a piano.

And then, there was one last question burning in Pru's head:

What was she going to do?!

Obviously, the musical instrument

idea was out now. It would be too weird if she and Catalina had the same act. And Pru recognised the determination in Catalina's eyes. She often had that same look and it meant just one thing: Catalina *would* get Milton to play – eventually. He'd play the piano and he'd play it well ...

Pru also had to admit that although a horse creating music was still the best idea she had, Boomerang wouldn't play along – that's why she'd been looking for alternatives.

She needed something as good as the music idea, but not the music idea!

This was frustrating and terrible and there was so much pressure.

Pru ran back to the corral, where her friends were waiting.

'Chica Linda is a happy horse,' Solana reported.

'It's curry time,' Abigail said. She rubbed

her belly. 'I can't wait to taste it.' She quickly added, 'Again.'

'I can't go,' Pru told them all.

'Why not?' Lucky asked. 'You'll miss the fun.'

'Catalina has a good act idea. Better than mine. She'll win for sure.'

'It's not a competition,' Lucky tried to remind her, but in Pru's mind it was a full-on competition now!

'I gotta do better. I gotta get Lydia Sebastian to write about me. I gotta get in the newspaper so my whole family can see.' Pru climbed over the corral fence and whistled for Boomerang. 'I'm going to work here with Boomerang – all night if I have to – until I come up with a great idea.'

Diary Entry

Dear Diary,

1. Fall down more.
2. Get hit by pie — a small pie for me and a big one for Boomerang.
3. Read Boomerang a book.
4. Cancel the show.

It's getting so hard to come up with anything new. All I want to do is go back to the 'horse plays music' idea, which again, wasn't great and didn't work — but it's as if that is the only idea stuck on an endless loop in my head.

Last night, after I had my freak-out, my very good, best friends stayed awhile to help me with ideas, but Abigail's stomach kept rumbling and I could see Lucky looking over her shoulder at all the festivities going on.

I gave up.

My stomach was rumbling, too and we weren't getting any closer to a genius idea.

We all decided that we needed to go out. We needed to eat. We needed to have a fun night.

And it was really fun.

We ate the curry and the spanakopita and something from the Middle East called falafel, which was like little fried balls of yumminess in a soft and delicious sandwich bread called a pitta. I liked the creamy sauce, too.

Abigail is collecting recipes. When we get back home to Miradero, she's going to make a feast. We can all help — well, I'd like it if the horses didn't cook, but I'm not sure that's a fight I'll win. Apparently Chica Linda is getting to be quite the chef's assistant while Boomerang is with me.

When we were full up to the brim, we went back to our own caravan area and everyone said goodnight. The second they all left me, I climbed onto Boomerang's back, stared into space and tried to come up with something good.

When my friends found me the next morning, Boomerang and I were both asleep in the saddle.

CHAPTER 5

The opening ceremony of the circus was held in the biggest tent that Pru had ever seen. It was created by linking several of the smaller circus tents together, so it had kind of a mismatched feel to it, like a huge billowing patchwork quilt.

The evening began with a parade.

'I'm here!' Pru waved at Abigail and Lucky from the stands. Since Pru was doing an exhibition act, she wasn't in the parade, but her friends were. They were carrying the flag of *El Circo Dos Grillos* in the welcome pageant. Solana was with them. She was riding her own horse, Luna, and was carrying a candle.

Pru had finished practising early with Boomerang because Abigail needed to get him ready. That worked out fine, because she wasn't really practising much anyway, more like staring at Boomerang, hoping the horse might have a clever idea for their performance. Boomerang wasn't helpful. He ate the grass while Pru wrote terrible, horrible, rotten ideas in her diary. She'd actually ripped out the page in the end, because there was nothing good on it.

Shaking off the feeling that she'd wasted the day, Pru found a seat in the front row of the stands. She wanted to be close to the action, where her friends could hear her cheer. She planned to be the loudest!

There was an empty seat next to Pru.

'Can I sit here?' a woman asked politely.

Pru glanced up to see Lydia Sebastian

standing over her, pointing at the spot on the bench.

'*Uhhh,*' She felt so uncomfortable, as if she were talking to a big celebrity. She steadied her nerves because this was a good opportunity to talk to the reporter, without Catalina. In fact, Pru took a good look around: Catalina wasn't anywhere in sight. It was a big tent, but still ... Pru didn't think she was at the celebration.

Lydia introduced herself.

'I'm Pru,' Pru replied. Since they'd never met before, she added, 'I'm the clown act for *El Circo Dos Grillos.*'

'I look forward to seeing your act,' Lydia said. There was a kindness in her voice that made Pru smile. 'Got anything special planned?'

'Sure,' Pru said, pinning a smile on her face. 'Lots of things. Big things. Interesting things. Big and interesting things.' Ack. She was sounding more like Abigail than herself. Pru tried to relax.

'That all sounds great,' Lydia told her. 'I'm a reporter,' she said, as if Pru didn't know already. 'Maybe I'll write about you in the paper.'

Pru held up two fingers and twisted them together. 'Hope so.'

Pru was trying to think of something else to talk about, when loud music suddenly filled the tent.

'It's starting,' Lydia said, taking out a pen and paper from her bag. 'I love the opening ceremony, don't you?'

'I've never been to a gathering like this before,' Pru admitted. 'My friends are in the parade, but I don't know what else to expect.'

'It's not a normal parade,' Lydia told her. 'Be prepared to be surprised!'

Lucky and Abigail hadn't told her about

anything special they were planning. But then again, Pru had been pretty absorbed in her own act and worries. Now she wondered what Lydia was talking about. She leaned forward in her seat as the flaps at the back of the tent opened and the opening ceremony exhibition began.

Lydia was right. This wasn't a normal parade. Pru had thought that everyone would just march around the ring, on foot or horseback, waving flags and cheering for the circuses. But it wasn't like that at all.

From the instant the tent flaps opened, acrobats came in flipping cartwheels. They leaped and tumbled and landed on one another's shoulders, making a human tower five people high!

'Which circus is that?' Pru asked Lydia.

Lydia grinned. 'They're all from different circuses! That's the best part.'

95

Pru couldn't believe she didn't know that there had been groups meeting from mixed-up circuses to put on their shows today. Had Lucky and Abigail been working with other groups? Pru realised she didn't always know what they were doing when she was practising with Boomerang.

Above her head, trapeze artists began swinging. Pru could see now that this was also a mixed-up circus group. No one had the same costume on and yet, they were fabulous!

Lydia said, 'They can't do the most impressive tricks here, because those take time to learn, but flipping and catching off the trapeze bars into the arms of someone you barely know is really impressive!'

Pru agreed. The same went for the tightrope acts – they didn't do their hardest stuff; they saved that for their main performance during the weekend, but the trust the performers showed to their counterparts in other circuses was incredible. *El Circo Dos Grillos* had amazing tightrope walkers, including Solana. Solana wasn't performing, but her parents were there, high above the audience. They shared the spotlight with performers from four other big tops and everyone cheered!

When it was time for the flags, Lucky led the way. She was holding their circus flag and standing, one foot on Chica Linda and one on Spirit. Pru had seen Lucky do tricks like this a thousand times, but when she flipped over and jumped, still standing, onto a strange horse that had moved in next to her – a horse from another circus – Pru was so impressed that she jumped to her feet and cheered.

Spirit didn't allow other riders on his back, so he stayed beside Lucky. But Chica Linda

let a boy from the Russian River Circus ride
her and then the rider leaped from horse
to horse while moving. The boy landed,
firm footed, on a black stallion and a new
girl landed on just one foot, balanced on
top of Boomerang. Abigail had started on
Boomerang herself and then suddenly was
riding the stallion. Pru hadn't even seen her
move there, it was so fluid.

The horses stayed together, riding fast
and in unison, while the riders played
leapfrog on their backs. It was dangerous
and exhilarating. All the riders held tightly
to their circus's flag and the horses were
dressed in the circus's colours.

Suddenly there was a loud cheer from
the seat next to her and Pru saw that Lydia
was also standing and cheering. Pru had
thought she'd be the loudest, but Lydia was
good cheer competition! They stood together,

shouting and howling and clapping and – through their similar enthusiasm – becoming friends. By the time Lucky landed back on Spirit and Abigail swung up onto Chica Linda, Pru and Lydia were hugging each other, jumping up and down together.

'That was the most amazing horseback riding I've ever seen!' Lydia said, making notes on her paper as the horses and riders passed them and rows and rows of trained dogs came barking past.

Pru smiled. 'The rider in front was my friend Lucky with her horse, Spirit.' She pointed to Abigail, now sitting back on Chica Linda. 'And that's Abigail. We're the PALs: Pru, Abigail and Lucky,' she explained proudly.

'Maybe I can talk to them later?' Lydia asked. 'For the article? Would they be open to an interview?'

At first, Pru felt a little pang of jealousy. She hadn't considered that Lucky and Abigail might get in the newspaper. Would there be room for all of them? How could she make her parents proud if she wasn't in the paper?

But then, as quickly as the jealous feelings came, they left. 'I'd be happy to introduce you!' she said. 'You should meet all the horses, too!'

Diary Entry

Dear Diary,

Lucky and Abigail said they wanted to surprise me with the show and boy was I surprised! It was amazing. I was so proud of my friends, now I just want them to be proud of me as well.

We spent hours with Lydia. Once I got to know her better, she wasn't intimidating anymore. And there were some big surprises — like, she loves s'mores almost as much as Abigail does. They had

a little contest to see who could
eat more toasted marshmallows. I
love a challenge but was glad I
skipped that one!

After the food, we decided to
go to the corral and check on the
horses. Lydia doesn't ride, but
she loves horses, so she tagged
along with us.

Lucky started calling the
reporter 'Stomach of Steel'
Sebastian because she was feeling
totally fine after eating more
than thirty marshmallows, while
Abigail, who'd managed only one
more, was moaning, holding her
belly and insisting she needed to

lie down. We got to the corral and Abigail made herself a bed of hay.

She was babbling. 'Don't worry about me. I'll just lie here stuffed like a pillow. Lucky can have Boomerang if I explode. I can't move ... I'm never eating another marshmallow again!' Which we all knew wasn't true. 'Just leave me here till morning.' She was going on and on, while we went to put nighttime blankets on the horses.

Lydia took care of Boomerang for Abigail.

While we made sure the horses had enough hay and water, Lydia became super chatty, like Abigail. I hadn't realised how similar those two were!

Lydia told us that she'd always wanted to be a writer. Whenever she had a pencil or pen, she'd write — on chalkboards, paper, napkins, even walls if there wasn't anywhere else to put down her thoughts. When she got a chance to cover the circus, she jumped at the chance and, all these years later, still loved her job.

Abigail, who was listening to us talk, shouted from the hay

bales. 'I used to like writing, too, before I got so stuffed I couldn't lift my hands.' She wiggled to show us how her hands were weighted down. 'Miss Flores is going to be mad.'

I laughed.

Lydia said that the town she lived in was a lot like Miradero. Copper Springs has only one school, so older kids were in the same room with younger ones and their version of Miss Flores was Mrs Goldfarb.

Catalina and Lydia were in the school together — they were kind

of like Turo and Snips, where
Turo is the oldest kid at school
and Snips the youngest.

A couple of years ago, just as
Lydia was graduating, Catalina's
parents took her from school and
left Copper Springs to be in the
circus full-time. They'd kept
in touch.

Part of me worried that there
was no chance for me to be in
the paper. The bond between
Catalina and Lydia was strong.
She told us that there was
even a song they both loved and
whenever they saw each other,
they'd sing it and think of home.

I knew that song.
It goes like this:

The heartbeat of the stallion
   Nickers in the breeze.
The wind gallops in
   four-beat stride
And the herd calls through
   the trees!

I'd have sung it, but I felt
nervous around Lydia and didn't
want to be embarrassed.
   Though she didn't mean to
worry me, Lydia's stories put
me on edge. I know that I can
compete with Catalina in the

ring, but I can't compete with friendship. I glanced at Abigail, who was dramatically moaning and rolling around in the hay and Lucky, who was giving Spirit an apple. I understood the bonds of friendship and if I had to write an article about the PALs or someone else, I was pretty sure I'd pick the PALs.

I frowned.

Lydia noticed and assured me that she'd be an impartial judge of who gets into the paper. Knowing Catalina wouldn't give her an edge.

But then ... she added the one thing that stuck with me all night.

Lydia said that Catalina seems sad. Last year, when they met at the exhibition, Catalina was loving her life in the circus and couldn't stop talking about it.

But this year, she's quiet, withdrawn and always alone.

Catalina told Lydia that a lot of her circus friends had left the caravan to go to boarding schools or simply gone back home. She was one of the only girls her age still on the circuit. Apparently Catalina also asked Lydia if she'd

been back to Copper Springs. Lydia
had and told Catalina about the
haunted hotel, the abandoned mine
and the new playhouse that she'd
never seen.

Catalina had so many questions
about Copper Springs, it seemed
odd. Especially given how much she
used to love the circus. Lydia
wondered what was wrong.

And that made me wonder, too.

CHAPTER 6

'Want a marshmallow?'

Abigail burst into the room soon after Pru woke up, waving a half-empty bag in Pru's face.

'What?' Pru squinted at the bag, then at Abigail and finally at Lucky and Solana, who were standing at the foot of her bed. 'Ew. No.' She sat up and yawned. Pru asked Abigail, 'I thought you were never eating another marshmallow, ever.'

'That was yesterday. Today's a new day,' Abigail said happily, popping a sweet fluffy treat into her mouth.

'Rise and shine,' Solana said. She had Pru's clown costume in her hand. 'We're

111

here to help you get ready for the best clown exhibition ever.'

'It's going to be so great that you'll be in the paper and everyone will be talking about it for years,' Lucky said as Solana handed Pru the costume. 'Okay, maybe not years. And we really don't have an idea yet, but we are here to help!' From behind her back, Lucky surprised Pru with a plate of pancakes and a cup of steaming tea.

'We knew you'd want to work all day,' Abigail said. 'So eat up. We're ready to help!'

After they'd said goodnight to Lydia, Pru had fallen asleep late and had nightmares about getting into the ring and having it be like the old days, where she panicked and couldn't do anything. In her dreams, she just stood there, mouth agape, staring at the silent crowd. After a few minutes they began to boo. And boo. And boo. And boo.

It was the worst dream ever.

After she woke up, Pru tried to calm herself by thinking of something her dad might say in this situation, but all she could come up with was 'You gotta get back on the horse that threw ya.' It didn't apply to this situation. She wished he was here so she could ask him for advice.

And then, just as she was getting ready to write a letter home, her friends arrived – eager and ready to help. Pru couldn't stop smiling.

'Thanks,' Pru said, taking breakfast from Lucky. She ate it quickly and then put on her costume.

'Boomerang is dressed, too,' Abigail said as they went outside. There Boomerang was, wearing his own clown costume with his mane and tail braided. 'I made him extra pretty for you today,' Abigail said. 'He fussed at first, but I shared the marshmallows and now we're good.'

Boomerang burped and an uneaten marshmallow fell out of his mouth. Abigail scooped it up and put it back in the bag. 'I'll save that one for later,' she said.

'I convinced Estrella to let us have the practice tent for extra time today. Since so many acts have already gone, she agreed,' Solana said.

They made their way to the small tent and Pru set up the drums.

Boomerang rejected the idea of playing. Pru gave a look to Chica Linda. They had all heard her play, but she stepped back now, still unwilling to perform.

Spirit wasn't a musical kind of horse, so Pru didn't even bother to ask.

'Okay, new ideas, ' She tapped her forehead with a finger.

'Let's do what we'd do at home,' Lucky suggested.

Pru didn't understand.

'Just ride,' Lucky said. 'We're trying too hard to be different. Maybe something will come out of us all acting normal.'

Pru nodded and hopped up onto her own horse's back. It felt good to be back on Chica Linda and Pru leaned into the familiarity of riding her own steed. Chica Linda was made for competition. She loved racing and jumping nearly as much as Pru did. When Pru squeezed her legs and gave Chica Linda the signal to run, the horse went wild. She bucked up, as if cheering for the freedom and took off at a gallop around the ring.

There weren't many obstacles, but what she could find, Chica Linda rode around. Someone had left out two chairs and Pru and Chica Linda circled them like barrels. There was a stack of weights left by the strongman. Chica Linda jumped over those, as if over a fence. She wove through the acrobat's crates of costumes and then started around the circuit again.

Abigail and Boomerang set out after Pru and Chica Linda. Abigail hadn't told anyone, but Solana had sneakily helped her turn those marshmallows into little paintballs by dipping them in colourful dyes. Abigail started throwing them at her friends and her friends' horses. Solana was throwing more from the stands.

Pop. A blue splat hit Pru's cheek. She couldn't tell if it was from Abigail or Solana.

'Let's go, Chica,' Pru told her horse, hugging down tightly on her neck. 'Don't let them paint you!'

Lucky and Spirit joined the fun, with Lucky doing a trick and hanging to the side of Spirit's back. She managed to get close to Abigail and nab a few of the coloured marshmallows from the bag.

Lucky tossed the marshmallow paintballs at Abigail, who got hit with yellow and green. Dye dripped down her leg and onto Boomerang.

'I've got you, Pru!' Abigail threw two purple pellets, but instead of hitting Pru, tagged Chica Linda.

When the marshmallows ran out, Spirit was the only clean horse. The others were covered in dye.

They all slowed down and, laughing, rode over to where Solana had been watching.

'That was hysterical,' Solana said. 'You guys should do that in the act!'

'But …we're not clowns,' Abigail said.

'We're just trying to help Pru get in the paper,' Lucky said.

Pru studied her friends and their horses. There was no rule that said she had to perform alone … and it was an exhibition, so maybe …

She thought more about Solana's idea.

The paintballs were fun … but a whole clown act was more than just one thing. Could the PALs and all the horses do a show together? Just this once?

She leaned down to Chica Linda, who didn't want to clown around in the first place, but was now acting a lot like a clown horse, covered messily in dye and all. Pru whispered a plan into Chica Linda's ear and this time, her horse didn't refuse.

Diary Entry

Dear Diary,

There's a constant banging sound from across the camp. It sounds like a gong or maybe as if someone is banging on a frying pan. Whatever it is, the racket is keeping me awake.

I put a pillow over my head. I wadded up tissue and stuffed pieces in my ears to plug them. I sang to myself. Nothing is drowning out the sound.

Finally, I gave up. I might as well think about my new plan for the show, since it's coming up fast. In hours, really.

I'm thinking we should

AGH. I can't concentrate with that noise.

That's it, Diary! I am going to check it out.

Dear Diary again,

I woke up Abigail and Lucky. Actually, Lucky was already awake, but Abigail was snoring loud enough that it drowned out the banging sounds. It took a few tries to wake her up and when we finally got her, she was so drowsy she thought I was her mum and that Lucky was Boomerang.

Lucky played along, neighing, until Abigail figured out it was us and that her horse didn't have a cold.

We didn't even change out of pyjamas. It was dark, but there were lights in some of the tents, probably from other people who couldn't sleep. Using the lights and sticking to the shadows, we made our way towards the sound.

I was shocked.

And I was right. At least,
sort of. The noise <u>was</u> banging on a
frying pan. But it wasn't a someone
— it was a horse.

Catalina's horse.

'Come on, Milton, <u>shhhh</u> ... '
She was dressed as if she'd been
practising for the exhibition, but
there was bread in her hair, egg
yolk on her shirt, milk on her
face and something green all
over her pants. 'You're waking
everyone up. I need you to <u>cook</u>
the French toast, not bang on
the pan.'

(French toast doesn't have any green ingredients as far as I know. Ewww.)

I thought we should hide, but Abigail stepped out of the shadows and told her that if she wanted to teach Milton to cook, she was making a lot of mistakes.

Catalina jumped a little, surprised that anyone was there.

Abigail plowed forward, explaining that she'd taught two horses to cook now. Three if we counted her brother Snips's donkey as a horse, which wasn't entirely accurate, since donkeys aren't horses.

I nearly gagged when she said that Señor Carrots made an excellent carrot cake, because I've eaten that cake. And while it is pretty good, I won't be eating it ever again.

Lucky pulled Abigail back into the shadows, while Abigail complained she just wanted to help.

Catalina then got mad and told us she didn't want help. She took the frying pan away from Milton.

Someone shouted for us all to be quiet. So we left. Catalina took Milton and stormed off

towards her own caravan and we
went back to ours.

Diary, I'll tell you this one last
thing before I go back to sleep:
Lydia was right. Catalina seems
very sad. In fact, I'm not sure
I've ever seen her happy.

CHAPTER 7

'Pru, rise and shine!' Abigail was standing over Pru's bed.

'Neigh!' Lucky tried to sound like Chica Linda.

'You can't fool me,' Pru told Lucky, laughing. 'But nice try.' She yawned and checked the time. 'Oh, wow. Thanks for getting me up. Since Lydia's going to be working on her article tonight, there's a lot to do before the performance.' The clown exhibition was one of the final shows before the closing ceremony. Tomorrow, the circuses would all pack up and be back on the road.

Pru looked at her friends. They were both

ready for the day. 'You're going to practice with me, right?' Pru asked. 'We're in this together now.'

'Of course,' Lucky assured her. 'It's going to be the greatest clown exhibition ever.'

'We'll all be in the newspaper,' Abigail said, feeling certain. 'My mum and dad will be so surprised. And then I bet Snips will proudly take our article and run around town, gushing about us and showing everyone, like Turo and Maricela and Miss Flores and Mr Winthrop, too,' She paused and shrugged. 'Or Snips might just use the paper to clean his boots. It could go either way.'

Pru got dressed and ready for the day. 'So what's got you two so excited to wake me up?'

'Well,' Lucky said, stalling a little and blocking the door to the outside.

'We found your letter,' Abigail blurted out.

At Lucky's glance she said, 'Sorry, Lucky. You were just talking so slowly.'

'What letter?' Pru asked. 'I didn't write—' Then she remembered. 'I thought I lost that.'

'It was in Boomerang's saddlebag,' Lucky said, bringing the letter out from behind her back.

Abigail took the letter and said, 'Sorry, Pru. We didn't realise it was private until we hit the green-bean part.' She sniffled. 'It was so touching.'

Pru wasn't mad they'd read her letter. They were her friends and meant well.

'Are you still homesick?' Lucky asked.

'Not really,' Pru admitted. 'But we've been so busy with the exhibition and everything, I kind of forgot about it.'

At that, Abigail frowned. Then her face lit up. 'Well, okay. In case it happens again, we made you a surprise!' Abigail said.

'Surprise?' Pru echoed cautiously. She didn't really like surprises all that much.

Lucky moved away from the door and Abigail opened it.

Pru peeked out. 'Am I supposed to see something?'

'Oh yeah,' Abigail said. 'We have to walk to the corral.' She grinned sheepishly.

They led Pru the short distance to the corral. There was a big curtain at the side of the fence. It blocked Pru's view.

'Where are Chica Linda, Boomerang and Spirit?' she asked. 'Are they all right?'

'Ta-da!' Abigail and Pru cheered as Solana stepped around the curtain and pulled it aside.

'Oh wow!' Pru felt tears in her eyes as she saw what her friends had done.

Using wooden boards, they'd created stalls for the horses. And not just any stalls, but they'd decorated them to look *exactly* like the barn at home. The horses were each in their stall, looking happy and gazing at Pru as if they'd helped with the surprise.

'I can't believe it,' Pru said, rushing up to Chica Linda for a hug. She was under her nameplate, just as if they were at home. She gave loving rubs to Spirit and Boomerang, too.

'You guys!' Pru gushed. 'You're the best friends I could ever have.'

'We're better than best,' Lucky assured her. 'There's more.'

'Okay, so we know it's breakfast time, but because of the practice today and the show later, we didn't have another time to do this, so – surprise!' Abigail reached down and took a pan out of a small bag. She set the pan on a nearby picnic table and swept off the cover with flair.

'Is that my mum's green-bean casserole?'
Pru held back another wave of
happy tears.

'I had the recipe,' Abigail said proudly. 'We
didn't have all the ingredients, so it's almost
your mum's casserole.'

Pru hugged Abigail. 'I never really liked it
anyway. It just reminded me of home.'

They all laughed.

'Oh, good then,' Lucky said, getting
another pan out of the bag. 'We can have
eggs instead.'

'Boomerang and I made the casserole,'
Abigail protested. 'We're all eating it. In
honour of Pru's big show.'

No one refused and the truth was, the
casserole was better than Pru's mum had ever
made it.

'You all made the circus feel just like
home,' Pru said before eating another bite

of the casserole. 'Thank you so,' Her voice faded. She stared at the beans on her fork.

'What?' Abigail asked. 'Do you feel okay, Pru? I mean, I picked wild mushrooms, but the cook promised they were the good kind, not the poison kind.' She put a hand to her forehead. 'Oh no! We made this nice surprise and I poisoned my friends.' She started to collect plates. 'No one eat the casserole!' Abigail rushed to take back the plate she'd given to Boomerang.

'It's not that,' Pru said. 'No poison. All is fine. Good. Great.' She paused as her thoughts came together. 'It's just that the casserole and the stalls – it made me think of something.' She got up and gave Lucky the rest of her food. 'Save this for me. I'll be right back!'

And with that, Pru ran away.

Diary Entry

Dear Diary,

From my first bite of green-bean casserole, I knew what was wrong with Catalina. It wasn't that she also couldn't come up with something newspaper-worthy for the exhibition.

Lydia had said that Catalina seemed sad. I understood that and recognised the symptoms. That same sadness had been inside me, too, but I had friends to get me through the days and make things

fun and exciting. Catalina didn't
have friends to help her. She
was homesick and all alone.

I ran all the way to her circus
tent. Not knowing where she'd
be, I called her name from the
centre of the caravan.

No answer.

Then I heard a bang and crash
from the practice tent and I was
certain that I knew who made
that noise. I hurried there.

Peeking inside, I saw Catalina
standing by herself in the centre
of the ring. Milton was at the
far edge, eating oats from
a bucket.

Catalina caught my eye as I entered and stopped humming. She told me she was quitting.

I didn't understand why she'd do that.

She told me it was because Milton was being stubborn and she was out of ideas. Then she added that way back, when we'd first met and she told me she'd seen my show, that it wasn't as bad as she made it out to be.

Inside, I knew that meant she thought I was good, but I didn't let it go to my head.

I sounded like Lucky when I told her it wasn't a competition,

but neither of us believed that.
We were so similar, Catalina
and me.

We both grabbed on to a 'you
gotta be the best' idea and
neither of us had let go.

I asked her to come with me.
She said no.

I asked again. She protested.

I begged.

It went back and forth like
that for a long time. We were
pretty evenly matched in our
stubbornness. But then, Lucky and
Abigail and Solana and Spirit and
Chica Linda and Boomerang all
showed up.

It had taken Lucky and Abigail a few minutes to understand why I'd run off. But they got it, just like I thought they would. And when they realised what was up, they followed me. Just like I hoped they would.

Catalina didn't want to come along with us and at first Milton refused, too.

Being the leader of a herd back home, Spirit knew what to do. He herded her horse. It was amazing to watch the way Spirit circled Milton a few times at a gallop, leading him gradually towards the others. Milton seemed

uninterested at first, but Spirit
didn't give up. With his head
down, he continued to move
around Milton.

Chica Linda and Boomerang
raced along with Spirit and began
to whinny in welcome. Eventually
Milton decided to join the fun.
They all made a few circles
together around the ring before
settling down to head out.

My friends and the horses then
helped me rustle up Catalina. It
was a lot easier now that Milton
was on our team.

We got on horseback and invited
her to come along. When she

refused, Milton helped us
by nudging Catalina with his
nose. When she still refused, all
the horses joined the nudging.
Catalina was surrounded by horse
noses! Finally, she started to
laugh. And then we all
laughed, too.

After all that, she decided to
come along to our camp and the
'Miradero' party there.

At the Miradero party, we
gave our reluctant friend some
green-bean casserole, made another
horse stall like the one she had
for Milton back home and then I
gave a presentation.

I wasn't nervous since I was with my PALs. I stood up on that picnic table. Everyone gathered around and I sang that song that Lydia had said Catalina liked. The one from Copper Springs. The one they always sang together.

A few bars into it, Catalina jumped onto the table and started singing, too.

Then Lydia, who'd been passing by, joined in.

I guess when I said I'd never sing with Lydia, I was wrong. We sang the whole song twice, ending with a loud and prolonged

rendition of 'And the herd calls
through the trees!'

It was an amazing morning.
Catalina smiled bigger and
warmer than I'd ever seen.

CHAPTER 8

A nd next up in the country circus exhibition is—' The announcer stopped. Pru's name was on the card and only Pru's name. But gathering in the centre of the ring were more clowns than the announcer had ever seen.

'The next act is – *clowns!*' he announced at last as he tipped his tall hat at Pru before stepping away.

'We are the CLAPS band!' Pru announced and the crowd cheered. That was every initial of all the girls. 'And we hope you'll all *claps* for us!' She grinned.

Pru caught Lydia's eye. She was in the front row, holding her pen and paper ready.

Pru winked at her and then stepped back.

In the centre of the ring was a piano, bucket drums and a frying pan.

Pru and Catalina were dressed as if they were clown conductors.

Abigail, Lucky and Solana had a surprise for the audience.

Pru sighed. They were putting everything they had into this one performance.

Catalina did a cartwheel and the show began. First was some chasing around, getting the horses to the instruments. The girls fell over one another, knocking one another down. Lucky did a flip from Spirit onto Milton and the crowd went crazy. Then Chica Linda went to play the drums.

'Before I met you, I had no idea she liked music!' Pru whispered to Catalina. 'Thanks for showing me. And getting her involved!'

'Sure,' Catalina said with a shrug, as if it were all part of her plan all along.

When the *boom-boom* beat of the drums began, the other horses took their spots.

The girls had already seen that Milton loved banging his head on the frying pan. So now they covered it with soft material. The clang was still loud and rhythmic, but they weren't worried about him hurting himself.

Lucky was going to play piano. She wasn't great at it, but she was playing in a horse band. She'd sat down at the keyboard when suddenly she got nudged off the bench. The audience clapped, as if this were part of the show. Lucky laughed.

'Spirit?' She looked up as her wild stallion began to clomp his foot up on the keyboard. 'Okay,' Lucky said to him. 'The piano is yours.'

Solana and Abigail were dressed in clown

144

costumes with big feet. Their instrument was the marshmallow slingshot. The slingshots were strung tightly and made a twang sound when fired. They had an extra one for Lucky.

While the animals played in the band, Solana and Abigail kept the beat, but also shot marshmallows into the audience (plain, not dyed, so people could eat them). It was chaos – and hysterical!

There was one facet of the act left.

The music swelled in the tent and the pops of the marshmallows filled the air. The crowd was on their feet, catching the treats and cheering.

Pru whispered to Abigail, 'Now I have a surprise for *you*.' She rushed to a curtain at the back of the tent and pulled it back dramatically to reveal Boomerang – dressed like a green unicorn!

Pru led Boomerang out to the centre of the

band and stood by him. 'Okay, Boomerang, time to sing.'

Nothing happened.

She turned to Abigail. 'You said he could sing.'

Abigail shrugged. 'Maybe just when he's taking a bath?'

'Oh.' That sort of made sense to Catalina. 'What are we going to do?' she asked.

'Let's sing,' Pru suggested. 'All of us.'

'But it's not the right tune,' Lucky pointed out. The horses were playing whatever they wanted.

'I don't think it matters,' Pru said. 'It'll be funny!'

The band played one song. The clowns sang another. It was chaotic and hysterical.

'Whoa.' To Pru's ears, the music sounded like a cross between crying babies and howling monkeys.

The crowd loved it.

The performance was amazing. And when it was over, the audience begged for an encore.

They couldn't refuse.

After they'd finished, the PALs, Solana and Catalina were shocked to find that the autograph line stretched around the tent. It took more than an hour to greet all their new fans.

The last person waiting in line was Lydia Sebastian.

'Congratulations!' She gave high fives and hugs to each of the girls and sugar cubes to each of the horses. Lydia had a camera with her. 'You were by far the best act in the exhibition. I'll be writing my article about the clown act. Can I get a photo?' She had her camera with her.

The girls gathered around with all the horses. They were all still dressed in costume.

147

'Say 'cheese,'' Lydia Sebastian told them.

They all started to say it, but then Boomerang suddenly brayed loud and squeaky – it didn't sound like 'cheese,' but whatever it was, it made them all laugh.

Lydia snapped the camera and the moment was captured on film.

Diary Entry

Dear Diary,

Abigail and Lucky knew the truth all along: I never really made a wish on the green unicorn.

I thought it was silly and wishes like that never come true. But you know what? Everything I ever wanted really did come true at the circus exhibition. I had the most amazing clown show ever, I got to be in the newspaper, I wasn't homesick anymore and my best PALs were by my side. What more could I want?

Before we washed the paint off Boomerang and removed his costume, I brought him out and told my friends to make a new green-unicorn wish.

I held hands with Catalina while she whispered what was in her heart. 'I hope that we'll all be friends forever,' she said softly.

I leaned over to her and said, 'Yep. That's what I want, too.'

'Me too,' Solana said.

'Yep,' Lucky added.

'Friends forever,' Abigail finished. 'That's the perfect wish.'

Abigail, Lucky and Solana gathered around us. We all hugged and cried a little — knowing this wish would definitely come true.

Join Lucky on the next adventure!

DREAMWORKS

Spirit

RIDING FREE

NETFLIX
NOW A NETFLIX
ORIGINAL SERIES

LUCKY'S DIARY

By New York Times Bestselling Author
Stacia Deutsch

Kirkus calls **DreamWorks**
Spirit Riding Free: The Adventure Begins,

'A wild ride that will make spirits soar.'